D0461258

THE LEGEND OF STRAP BUCKNER

A Texas Tale

retold by

Connie Nordhielm Wooldridge

illustrated by

Andrew Glass

Holiday House / New York

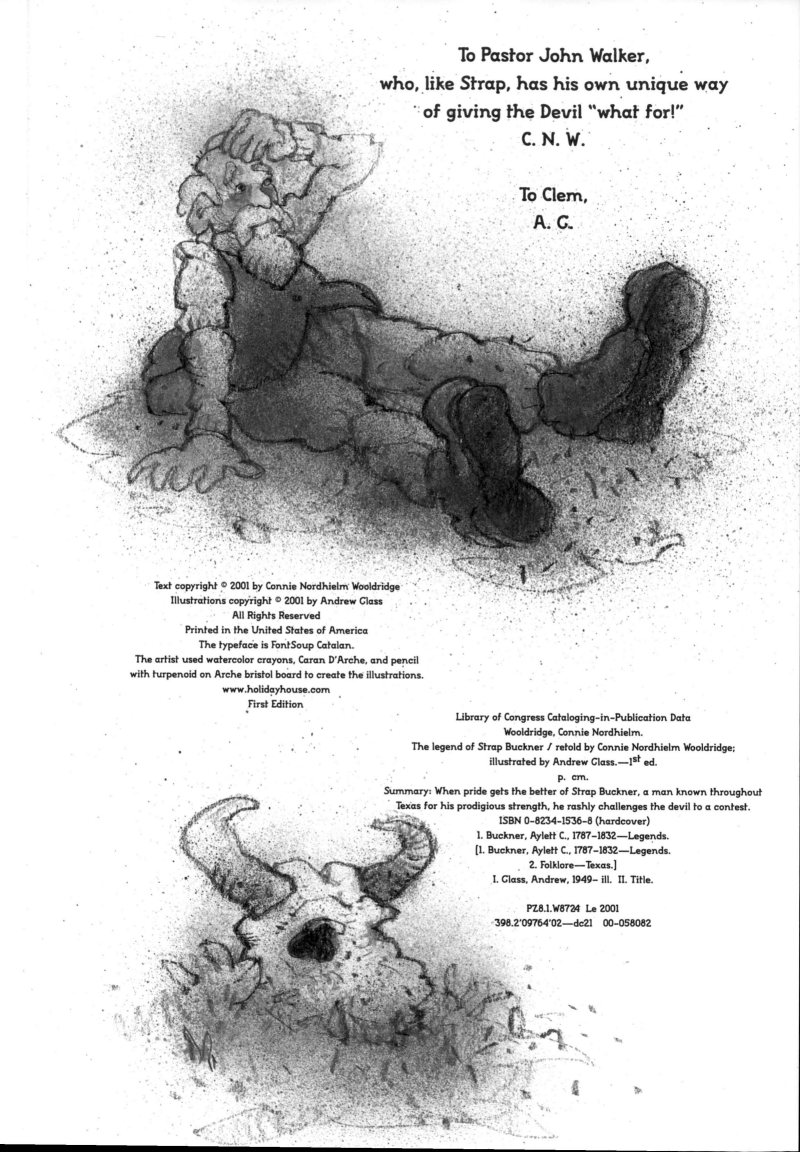

To Pastor John Walker,
who, like Strap, has his own unique way
of giving the Devil "what for!"
C. N. W.

To Clem,
A. G.

Library of Congress Cataloging-in-Publication Data
Wooldridge, Connie Nordhielm.
The legend of Strap Buckner / retold by Connie Nordhielm Wooldridge;
illustrated by Andrew Glass.—1st ed.
p. cm.
Summary: When pride gets the better of Strap Buckner, a man known throughout
Texas for his prodigious strength, he rashly challenges the devil to a contest.
ISBN 0-8234-1536-8 (hardcover)
1. Buckner, Aylett C., 1787–1832—Legends.
[1. Buckner, Aylett C., 1787–1832—Legends.
2. Folklore—Texas.]
I. Glass, Andrew, 1949– ill. II. Title.

PZ8.1.W8724 Le 2001
398.2'09764'02—dc21   00-058082

STRAP BUCKNER was
a man of genius...

...and his genius was to knock folks down.

When Stephen F. Austin showed up here in Texas with three hundred families wanting to settle, Strap knocked them down, one by one, as way of saying welcome. He even knocked down the great Austin himself so he wouldn't feel left out.

Because his spirit was as gentle as his strength was great, he took any who were scratched or bruised in the knocking-down back to his cabin and tenderly nursed them back to health.

Then, with an air of unspeakable
grace, he knocked them down again.

Strap began to notice the folks of San Felipe steering clear of him. There's some would conclude this was because they were plain tired of getting knocked down. But that would be an ordinary thought and not one that would grace the mind of Strap Buckner.

"It is ever thus with a man of genius!" he lamented. "To be misunderstood, shunned, avoided by the common folk of the world!" A great salt tear rolled down his cheek, bounced off the toe of his boot, and knocked down an insect that was happening by. He resolved to leave San Felipe.

"Fare thee well, Strap Buckner," called the settlers from behind doors shut tight.

"Farewell to thee, San Felipe!" Strap bellowed tenderly.

He traveled west. After many adventures too numerous to relate, he happened on a solitary trading house, at which place Bob Turket and Bill Smotherall were engaged in swapping goods with the Indians of the area. His heart swelled at the sight of human company, and he forthwith knocked down Bob Turket, Bill Smotherall, and every Karankawan brave within a ten-mile radius. He even knocked down Chief Tuleahcahoma so he wouldn't feel left out. The chief was so impressed he named Strap "Red Son of Blue Thunder" and presented him with a horse that was ugly and lank to look at but swifter than a Texas wind.

Strap built himself a cabin of cedar posts and settled in with his swift gray nag. Daily he went forth and knocked men down with great grace.

But the day came when he went forth and met with not a soul. The settlers of the area had slipped away in the dead of night, leaving him alone and desolate. He wept for two days pondering the price of his genius. "Like a towering mountain I stand alone!" he wailed. "Such is the penalty of my greatness!"

Into the middle of his wailing came the voice of his better spirit: "Strap! Hast thou not glory enough? Hast thou not knocked down nearly every man in Texas? Forsake thy genius and seek peace, gentle peace!"

Strap smiled and raised his arms heavenward. He resolved to live in peace with all humanity.

But the Devil never can let a man's good resolve go unchallenged. That very day, he devised a mighty temptation: Riding along on his swift gray nag, Strap came upon twenty-two Karankawan braves holding a meeting right there in front of his newly peaceful self.

Strap stepped into the middle of the gathering and bowed
nobly. He thought on his greatness (which, his better spirit
reminded him, was enough) and he thought on gentle peace
(which, his better spirit reminded him, was sweet).

And then his genius overcame both those goodly thoughts and erupted like a volcano. He let out a whoop and knocked the braves down, one by one. With never a thought to their scratches and bruises, he leaped astride his swift gray nag, galloped to the trading house, and knocked down Bob Turket at the door and Bill Smotherall as he tried to escape.

His erupted genius broke all bounds in its quest for glory and greatness in the eyes of all men.

He sprang to the counter and smote the air with his iron fists: "Behold in me the Champion of the World! I challenge any man to take me on!" he crowed. "I wager my swift gray nag! Who will take the wager? I challenge the old Devil himself!"

No sooner were the words spoken than a dark rumbling sound issued from the forests round about. It swelled and grew till it rattled the earth below and the heavens above. Strap leaped on his swift gray nag and rode back to his cabin.

By the time he reached home, the rumbling sound had become a storm that pounded his cabin walls with the force of an evil invasion. There came from without a concussion so violent it appeared the very hills were being toppled. When Strap recovered from the sound, he beheld on the floor before him a sinister figure—not three feet high—with two red horns and the cloven hooves of a bull. His face showed great age and infinite villainy. It was the Devil himself.

"Thou hast challenged me, Strap Buckner, and wagered thy swift gray nag," he said. "I accept thy challenge to a duel: tomorrow morning at nine o'clock, under yon oaks. Give us thy hand on it, Strap Buckner. Skin for skin!"

They clasped hands and shook. The Devil shrank up and departed through the keyhole, leaving a mighty smell of brimstone in his wake.

"Tomorrow the world will sing of my glory!" Strap crowed. His pride blinded him to the notion that things just might go another way. He lay down to sleep while the elements waged war outside his cabin walls.

Day had a time of it trying to dawn. When it finally succeeded, Strap put on his buckskin garment, whistled to his swift gray nag, and sallied forth. "The hour has arrived," he said.

The Infernal Fiend was immediately before him. "I will lead and thou wilt follow!" he said. He marched on before with his tail coiled over one arm till he reached a cluster of oaks bearded with moss. "Now is the hour and here the place!" he announced.

Strap turned his swift gray nag loose to graze and faced
his evil adversary. He found the Devil grown to enormous
proportions. He towered over Strap and twirled his tail in
the storm-blackened sky till it stuck fast in a cloud.

"Thou art a coward to fight me on such
unequal terms!" protested Strap. "Regain
thy size and I will lay aside my only weapon!"
Strap tossed aside his iron pestle and
the Devil shrank.

Only thing was, he forgot about his tail hitched to the cloud and he found himself dangling from the sky upside down, blown backward and away on the wind. It was the Hand of Providence offering Strap one last chance to admit he might need a Strength bigger than his own to win this one. Once again he was blind to the very notion.

"I will conquer thee with my own great strength and with help from neither man nor Providence!" he vowed. He used one iron fist as a springboard for the Devil and gave a mighty heave. The Devil coiled up to the cloud and unhooked his tail. When he bounced back to earth, he saw pride in Strap's eyes and heard the echo of it in his boast. There's nothing weakens a man who's facing the Devil more than pride, and nobody knows that better than the Devil himself.

"Skin for skin, Strap Buckner," he said. And the battle commenced.

Back at the trading house, Bob Turket and Bill Smotherall listened all day to the tangled-up noises of the fearsome storm and the hideous battle.

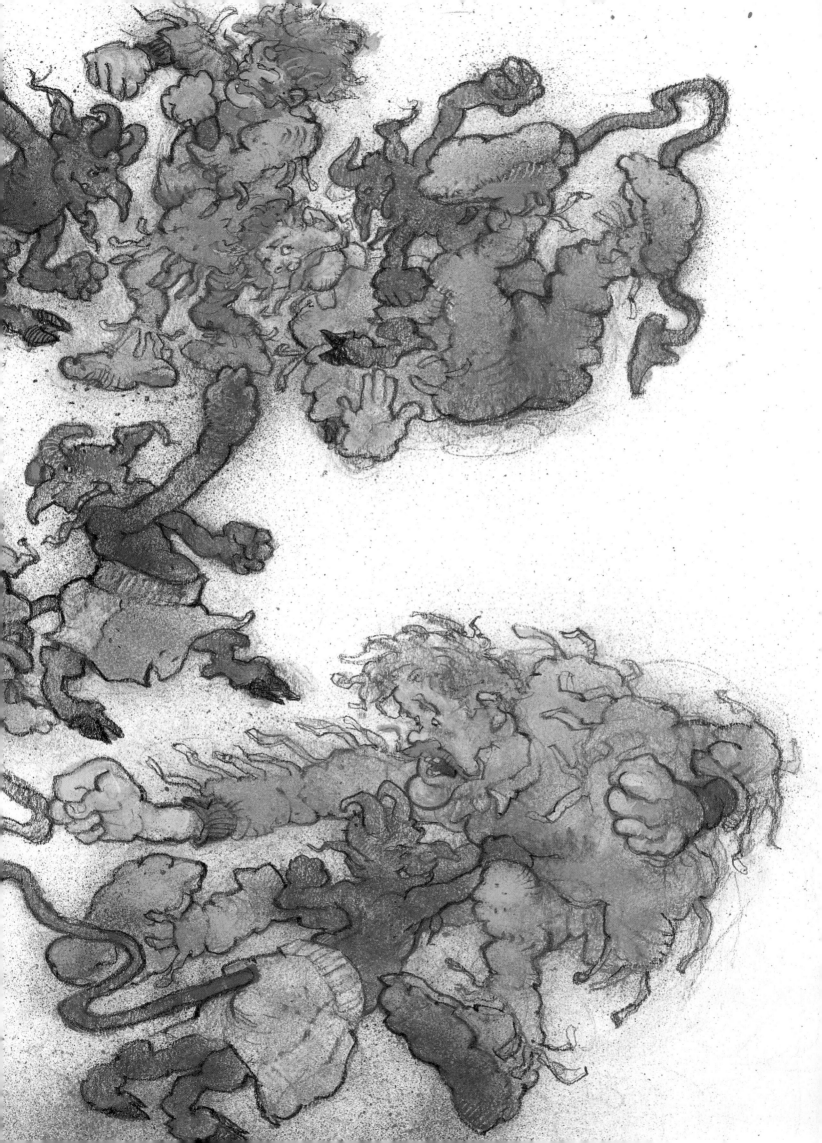

Toward evening, quiet fell and they dared to crack the door
and look out. They beheld a swift gray nag riding through the
sky with a villainous form in the saddle. Flung across the
back of the horse was the worn-out figure of a man.

Nothing was seen or known of Strap for upward of three months. Then one day, he appeared out of nowhere, riding through the settlement on his swift gray nag. He went about his business as if things were just like normal, but he was changed: He knocked no man down and not a boastful word fell from his lips. After a time, he disappeared again as mysteriously as he'd come.

Bob Turket and Bill Smotherall claimed they spotted him one last time after that. According to them, they saw a great blue flame rise over the valley. On top of the flame was a horse and on top of the horse rode a gigantic man with bright red hair, waving an iron pestle. On the horse in front of him was that very same villainous form cowering in fear.

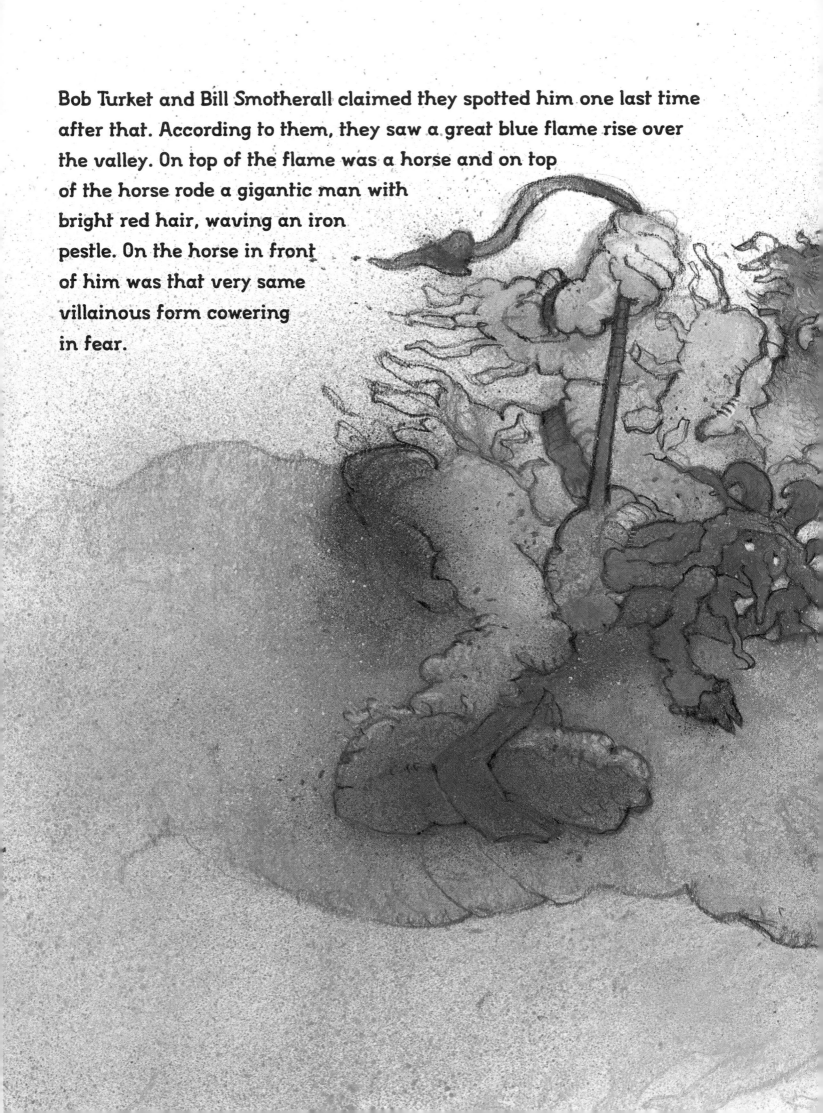

Who's to know if Bob Turket and Bill Smotherall are telling the truth? But if they are, it could just be that Strap finally came to know that the thing that really needed knocking down was his own pride. And it could just be, once he realized that, he gave the Old Devil what for!

AUTHOR'S NOTE

STEPHEN F. AUSTIN

Aylett C. (Strap) Buckner settled in what is now Fayette County, Texas, in 1819. Four years later, Stephen F. Austin showed up with some three hundred families and official permission to settle the area. Austin convinced Buckner to move to what was probably an inferior piece of land, and the two were at odds with each other for several years. At one point Buckner organized a protest and Austin commissioned one Andrew Rabb to arrest him for "disorderly and seditious conduct against the authorities of the government." Mr. Rabb knew how Strap had come by his nickname: He was a red-haired giant of a man who stood six and a half feet tall and weighed 250 pounds. Rabb came down with a mysterious ailment before he could carry out his assignment! Buckner and Austin finally settled their disagreements and became friends. Strap Buckner is duly listed as one of the venerable "Old Three Hundred" original settlers.

Strap Buckner stands beside such colorful Texas characters as Brit Bailey and Roy Bean. His prodigious strength and his habit of welcoming new colonists with a slap on the back that sent them flying grew into a host of legendary tales involving bare-handed combat with fierce animals and a duel with the Devil himself. Together, the factual and legendary parts of his life provide a window into that ornery but warm energy that is uniquely Texan.

Bibliography

STRAP BUCKNER THE LEGEND

Dobie, J. Frank, ed. *Legends of Texas.* Hatboro, PA: Folklore Associates, 1964.

Shay, Frank. *Here's Audacity! American Legendary Heroes.* New York: Books for Libraries Press, Inc., 1967.

Taylor, Colonel Nathaniel Alston. *The Coming Empire; or, Two Thousand Miles in Texas on Horseback,* rev. ed. Dallas: Turner Company, 1936.

STRAP BUCKNER THE MAN

Brazoria County Historical Museum. http://www.bchm.org/Austin/colonial.html

Davis, Joe Tom. *Legendary Texians,* vol. II. Austin: Eakin Publications, 1986.

Dobie, J. Frank. *The Flavor of Texas.* Dallas: Dealey and Lowe, 1936.